# The Santa Trap

**About the author and illustrator:**

**Jonathan Emmett** was an architect before turning his hand to writing. Since then he has written many books for children – and won awards for them too. This story was inspired by the real Santa traps that Jonathan built as a boy!

**Poly Bernatene** has illustrated over sixty books for children in many countries all over the world. When he isn't busy illustrating, Poly works as a professor in the school in Argentina where he trained as an illustrator. He lives with his wife and two children, and has never tried to trap Santa.

For my father
for helping me hone my trapping skills
and with apologies to the rest of my family
for disturbing their sleep – J.E.

For my parents . . . and for Santa Claus! – P.B.

First published 2009 by Macmillan Children's Books
This edition published 2014 by Macmillan Children's Books
a division of Macmillan Publishers Limited
20 New Wharf Road, London N1 9RR
Basingstoke and Oxford
Associated companies throughout the world
www.panmacmillan.com

ISBN: 978-1-4472-3699-3

Text copyright © Jonathan Emmett 2009
Illustrations copyright © Poly Bernatene 2009
Moral rights asserted

2 4 6 8 9 7 5 3 1

A CIP catalogue record for this book is available from the British Library.

Printed in China

# The Santa Trap

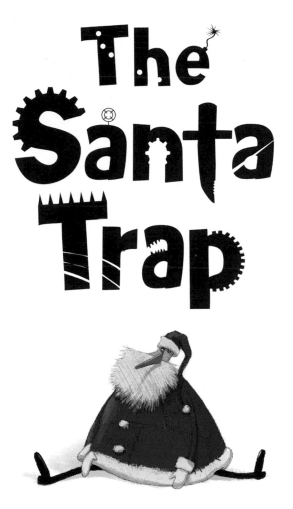

Jonathan Emmett

Illustrated by Poly Bernatene

MACMILLAN CHILDREN'S BOOKS

Bradley Bartleby was bad. He'd been born bad.

Before baby Bradley even left the hospital . . .

he'd bitten the midwife on the bottom, stolen the doctor's stethoscope, and emptied his nappy into his grandmother's handbag.

And the older Bradley got,
the badder he became.

Bradley's parents were immensely rich. They had a huge house with a garden that was big enough to lose an elephant in.

They knew that the garden was big enough to lose an elephant in because they'd done exactly that. Bradley had demanded the elephant as a house pet, but treated it so badly that it escaped into the garden and was never seen again.

Bradley's parents always gave him whatever he demanded, not because they thought he deserved it, but because they were terrified of him.

Every Christmas Mr Bartleby hired a team of secretaries to type up the huge list of presents that his greedy son demanded from Santa Claus.

Of course Santa knew what a beastly brat Bradley was, so he never looked at the list. But that didn't mean that he forgot about Bradley completely.

Santa is such a kind-hearted old fellow that he believes no child, even one as bad as Bradley, should go without a Christmas present.

So every Christmas morning Bradley would discover that Santa had left him the same small gift . . .

# "Socks!"

howled Bradley.
"Another pair of
stupid socks!"

"Never mind, Bradley dear!" cried Mr and Mrs
Bartleby, as they rushed in with a trolley-load of
presents. "Look, Mummy and Daddy have
got you everything you wanted."

"But I don't want presents from you!" roared
Bradley. "I want presents from Santa Claus, like
everyone else!" And he stormed back to his room.

The next morning Mr and Mrs Bartleby were alarmed to discover that their son had climbed up inside the living room chimney.

They were even more alarmed to discover that Bradley had nailed several sticks of dynamite around the chimney walls.

"What are you doing, dear?" asked Mrs Bartleby nervously.
"What does it look like?" scowled Bradley.
"I'm building a trap!"

"A trap," said Mr Bartleby. "A trap for what?"
"For Santa Claus," snarled Bradley. "I'm going to
catch the fat fool and take every present he's got."

Mr and Mrs Bartleby were speechless. In a lifetime of badness this was quite the baddest thing that Bradley had ever tried to do.

Mr Bartleby was the first to come to his senses. "Isn't it a little early to be setting a trap?" he gasped. "It will be a whole year before Santa comes again." "Oh, this is only the beginning," scoffed Bradley. "It'll take a whole year to finish it all."

And he was right. Bradley spent the rest of the winter fixing dynamite inside all the other chimneys . . .

and the spring training tigers, which he stole from the local zoo.

He spent the summer fitting guillotines over
all the doors and windows . . .

and the autumn cutting trapdoors into all
the floors.

By the time December came around again,
Bradley had turned the entire house into
one stupendous . . .

. . . Santa Trap!

By Christmas Eve their home was so dangerous that
Mr and Mrs Bartleby had moved out into a hotel,
leaving Bradley alone in the house!

"One last thing!"
said Bradley, as he hung
his stocking beside the fireplace.
He was certain that Santa
wouldn't make it that far, but just
to make sure he tied an invisible
tripwire to the stocking. The moment
anyone touched it a large metal
cage would drop down
from above.

"No more stupid socks!" thought Bradley.
"This Christmas, I'll get exactly what I want.
This Christmas, I'll get the whole lot!"

But as the evening grew darker, Bradley's eyelids
grew heavier. His evil efforts had left him quite
exhausted and he soon fell fast asleep.

It was almost midnight when Bradley was awoken by the roar of an angry tiger (whose tail had just been stepped on by an elephant). The house had grown chilly. And when he looked outside, Bradley was surprised to find the garden covered in a thick blanket of snow.

Shivering with cold, Bradley
decided to light a fire.

It was only when the flames began
to lick up the chimney

that Bradley remembered the dynamite . . .

# BOOM!

The explosion blew Bradley right through the living
room window and out into the rose bushes below.

Cursing loudly, Bradley struggled free of the thorny stems. He had barely caught his breath when six sleek, stripy shapes came bounding towards him out of the snow.

"Nice pussies," squealed Bradley as he fled back through the rose bushes with the tigers snapping at his heels.

The tigers chased Bradley around the garden twice before he was able to lose them (by diving into a heap of fresh elephant dung) and creep back to the house.

Determined not to be caught in any more of his own traps, Bradley took a deep breath and prepared himself before opening the front door.

**"Aha!"** he cried triumphantly, as he leaped clear of the falling guillotine.

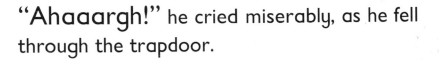

**"Ahaaargh!"** he cried miserably, as he fell through the trapdoor.

Some time later, as the sun rose on Christmas morning, a scratched, scraped and badly bruised Bradley limped back to the living room. There wasn't much of the fireplace left but, amazingly, his stocking was still hanging up.

And, even more amazingly, Bradley could see that there was something inside! Bradley hobbled over, tore down the stocking and . . .

# Clang!

The metal cage dropped right over him.

Bradley let out a long sigh. He knew that he was beaten. So he slumped down inside the cage and emptied his stocking onto the floor.

For the first time ever, Santa had left Bradley more than one present. There was a big box of bandages, a large jar of antiseptic and . . .

a nice new pair of socks!